5 Minute
DINOSAUR TALES
for
Bedtime

Illustrated by Peter Stevenson

Stories by Geoffrey Cowan, Andrew Farrow, Debbie Hendren, Wendy Hobson, Sri Lakshmi Hughes, David Kremer, Kim Kremer, Valerie Kremer, Sue Miles, Anne Sharples, Joanna Walsh and Jenny Walters

Derrydale Books
New York • Avenel, New Jersey

Editor: Kim Kremer
Designer: Gail M. Rose
Production: Mark Leonard

Illustrated by Peter Stevenson

Stories by Geoffrey Cowan, Andrew Farrow, Debbie Hendren,
Wendy Hobson, Sri Lakshmi Hughes, David Kremer, Kim Kremer,
Valerie Kremer, Sue Miles, Anne Sharples, Joanna Walsh, Jenny Walters

This 1994 edition published by Derrydale Books,
distributed by Random House Value Publishing, Inc.,
40 Engelhard Avenue, Avenel, New Jersey 07001.

Random House
New York · Toronto · London · Sydney · Auckland

ISBN 0-517-12019-4

Printed in Great Britain

Anton Quetzalcoatlus was a terrible flyer. When his friends saw him flying through the air, wings flapping crazily and feet outstretched, they would scatter as fast as they could before he crash-landed on them.

One day, a famous stunt master came to visit the neighborhood. It wasn't long before he saw Anton flapping about clumsily in the sky, and landing in a flurry of wings and squawks in the dirt. He laughed and laughed. "My!" exclaimed the great stunt bird. "I know why you have such trouble flying—you've got a tiny body, but your wings are enormous!"

"What can I do?" asked Anton, miserably.

"What can you do?" replied the stunt master. "With my help, you can be the greatest flyer on Earth with wings like that!"

And every day, Anton took flying lessons with the great stunt master, until he could fly with more grace and speed than the grand master himself. His friends were amazed to see the new Anton, swooping, diving, and looping fantastically through the air. Flying was no longer a painful way of getting around to Anton—it was his greatest joy in life.

Old Lizzie Stegosaurus was especially fond of large red tomatoes. She liked to eat them with cream, just like strawberries. Lizzie grew her tomatoes at the bottom of the garden, and was planning to enter them in the Pre-historic Garden Competition—she was very proud of her tomatoes and was determined to win first prize.

On the big day, Lizzie carefully gathered and polished the largest and roundest tomatoes. She put them on the judging table, and waited, nervously, for the results. "The winner," said the judge, "of the tomato competition . . . goes to Mr. Kritosaurus of Swampville!"

Lizzie was furious. She picked up her tomatoes, and swept out of the room. But then, she had a very naughty idea . . .

Lizzie slipped her tomatoes onto the strawberry table just as the strawberry judging began. "My!" exclaimed the judge, looking at the basket of tomatoes. "Those are the biggest strawberries I have EVER seen. I pronounce them the winners of this year's strawberry competition!"

Lizzie was delighted. "I knew he was extremely short-sighted," she thought. "Otherwise, he'd have known that no tomatoes are more beautiful than mine!"

Tilly was going to England to stay with her cousins. For at least the fifth time that afternoon she'd packed and repacked her own little suitcase. But she *still* couldn't get her toys to fit in, and she really did want to take all of them to show to her cousins.

Then she had an idea. Very carefully she opened her parents' suitcase, took out the top layer of clothes and replaced them with the rest of her toys. "They won't need all those clothes anyway!" Tilly thought.

The next morning, in England, Tilly awoke to the sounds of her father's angry roars. There he was, standing in the hallway, wearing nothing but his underwear! "My clothes have been stolen!" he cried.

"No they haven't," Tilly confessed.

She told the truth and her father, dressed in Uncle Ron's clothes, didn't seem so angry.

"Well," he said. "You'd better go and show your toys to William and Benjamin. It's caused a lot of trouble bringing them here!" He gave Tilly a big wink and then went to try on Uncle Ron's cricket cap.

Dinosaurs do not clean their teeth every night. In fact, they usually forget to clean them at all.

Harriet *never* cleaned her teeth, and this may have been the reason why she had such terrible toothache. It was so bad that Harriet couldn't sleep. Indeed, she roared with pain so loudly that everyone in the entire house woke up!

Harriet's mother comforted her and Harriet stopped roaring. Harriet's father went back to sleep. Grandma had an idea . . . She tied one end of a very long string to Harriet's tooth, and the other end to the open door. When Grandma shut the door, the string pulled tight and Harriet's tooth popped out! At last, the pain had stopped and everyone could go back to bed.

Of course, Harriet didn't mind losing a tooth because she still had one thousand, nine hundred and ninety-nine others!

etty hated shopping. Her mother had taken her to find a new dress to wear to her cousin Bettina's wedding.

"I hate dresses," said Letty. "Why can't I wear jeans?"

"You can't wear jeans to a wedding, Letty," said her mother. "Everyone else will be all dressed up. This is a lovely dress, Letty," she said, picking one off the rack. "Why not try it on?"

"I don't like frills," complained Letty.

"Well how about this one? It's such a nice color," said Mrs. Lesothosaurus, choosing another.

"I hate pink," pouted Letty.

"This one is very pretty," said her mother.

"Yuck! It's got bows," moaned Letty.

Letty didn't like any of the dresses in that store . . . or in any other store. . .

"Letty Lesothosaurus!" said her mother, finally. "I'm fed up with you. You can go and choose your own dress!" And she sat down on a street bench, exhausted.

Mrs. Lesothosaurus was astonished when Letty returned with a dress ten minutes later.

"But it's got *bows*," she said, "and *frills* and it's *pink*!"

"Yes, I know," replied Letty, "but it's made of denim—just like my jeans."

Tricky Ricky was a terror. His aunt had given him a big red crayon. Now Tricky Ricky scribbled on *everything*.

"Who's been writing on my new kite?" cried little Horace Hadrosaur (who was very upset.)

"Who drew on my nice clean wash?" growled Stan Stegosaur (who did all his own laundry.)

"Wait 'til I catch the monster who scribbled on my door!" threatened Stan's friend, Lawrence (who always made a lot of noise.)

But nobody could catch Tricky Ricky, because he could run even faster than Lightning Larry Lizard (who was very fast.)

One day Sneaky Cyril decided to teach Tricky Ricky a lesson.

"I can write my name bigger than you can," sneered Cyril, writing CYRIL all over a big rock.

"No you can't," said Tricky Ricky. He pulled out his crayon, hopped on a big stone, and wrote TRICKY RICKY on the biggest rock in the park.

But it wasn't a big rock. It was Terrible Tyrannosaurus Ted, and Tricky Ricky was very careful where he scribbled after that!

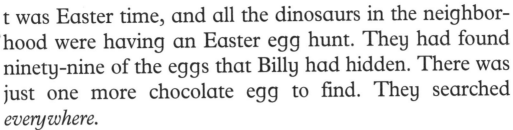

It was Easter time, and all the dinosaurs in the neighborhood were having an Easter egg hunt. They had found ninety-nine of the eggs that Billy had hidden. There was just one more chocolate egg to find. They searched *everywhere.*

"Am I getting closer?" asked Pedro Pentaceratops.

"Oh, you're *very* close," replied Billy. "The trouble is, of course, that this egg tends to move about a bit."

The dinosaurs were very puzzled. They looked under bushes and turned over stones. Ali even disturbed Mrs. Allosaurus' nest, and for a moment thought she'd found the egg she was looking for. "Not those!" cried Mrs. Allosaurus.

Finally, the dinosaurs said, "We give up. Tell us where it is!" Billy smiled. He went over to Pedro Pentaceratops, and pulled out the last chocolate egg from behind his bony neck frill.

"It's been just behind your nose all this time!" And he gobbled it up as quickly as he could, because the egg-hunters looked *very* annoyed!

Jasper Centrosaurus was the boxing champion of Fossil High School for Horned Dinosaurs. No one had ever managed to beat him, and so Jasper became very conceited, and sometimes, a bit of a bully.

One day, a new dinosaur came to the school. Her name was Meg Tiny Dino because she was very small. When Jasper began to bully her, Meg challenged him to a boxing match. "But I couldn't possibly fight with *you*!" Jasper laughed. "It would be far too easy to win." The dinosaurs tried to persuade Meg not to fight Jasper, but she was determined to teach him a lesson.

All the dinosaurs crowded into the playground to watch the boxing match. Jasper pulled the first punch, but before he could hit little Meg, she had dived straight for his ribs—Meg didn't punch Jasper, she tickled him!

"Hee hee hee," giggled Jasper. "Oh no, oh ha ha, stop! Please stop! I give up. You're the champion!"

Meg smiled, and all the dinosaurs cheered. "I knew you weren't as tough as you look," said Meg. "Promise never to bully anyone again, or I'll tickle you!" she threatened. And Jasper did promise—very quickly!

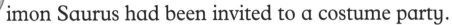

Simon Saurus had been invited to a costume party.

"I'd like to be a fierce monster," he decided. So Mom made some cardboard claws to fit over his hands and painted a fierce mask. Simon was not impressed.

"How will I eat my food?" he cried. "That's no good at all. I want to be a king instead."

Fortunately, the spiky claws looked like a crown when they were turned upside down, and a bedspread made a splendid cloak. Simon was still not impressed.

"How will I play running-around games with that cloak?" he complained. "I want to be an explorer."

Mom stuck the crown on the end of a stick for a spear. They found a backpack and a battered old hat. But Simon was not impressed.

"How will I play Pass the Package if I have to hold these?" he grumbled. "I want to be a . . ."

"No more!" said Mom. "You can make your own costume!"

When it was time to go, Simon appeared wearing the backpack on his chest, the long cloak, the monster mask on his tail, and the cardboard crown on his head.

"I'm a Sorry-osaurus," said Simon.

"Well, that's an excellent choice," laughed his Mom, and they were friends again.

It was Humbert's first day on the ski slopes, and he stood at the top of the mountain, looking down. It looked awfully steep. Just as he was wondering how on earth he was going to gather up the courage to ski down, he felt himself slipping . . . and before he could stop himself, Humbert was off down the mountainside, picking up speed as he went!

As he hurtled off, he heard someone shout, "Oh my goodness, he's heading for the ski jump!" And sure enough, he was . . .

"Aaargh!" roared Humbert, as he saw the ski jump ahead of him. Since he didn't have the faintest idea of how to stop himself, Humbert went sailing over the ski jump, shot into the air, turned head over heels, and landed with a thump at the bottom.

It took quite a while before Humbert's ski instructor reached the spot where Humbert was lying in a heap, with a bruised tail and a broken pole. "The first thing I'm going to teach you, Humbert," he said, "is how to stop!" But Humbert thought he'd had enough skiing for one day . . .

Alice Scelidosaurus was going to a party, and she wanted a new pair of shoes to wear. "Come along, Sylvester!" she said to her younger brother, who was busily painting a picture. "I'll need your advice on which pair of shoes to buy." The trouble was, Alice had VERY BIG feet. They went from store to store, but she couldn't find a single pair of shoes that were large enough.

Alice began to get rather annoyed. "All dinosaurs have big feet!" she complained. "Surely there must be *something* large enough for me? After all, I can't go barefoot to the party."

"I'm afraid your feet are even bigger than most," said Sylvester, who wanted to go home and finish his picture. "But I think I may have an idea . . ."

Alice *did* go barefoot to the party, but nobody knew, because Sylvester had painted a fabulous pair of shoes on Alice's feet. "Oh, Alice!" her friends gasped. "Where *did* you get your shoes?"

"Oh, I had them made especially for me," she said, and smiled sweetly.

Roland Styracosaurus was sitting in his math class, daydreaming as usual. He was thinking about what he would do if he won the lottery. Would he build a swamp adventure playground all for himself? Or, would he buy a chocolate factory? Perhaps he would travel the world in a private airplane . . .

"Roland!" shouted Mr. Megalosaurus, crossly. "I'm talking to you!"

Roland looked up in fright at the blackboard on which Mr. Megalosaurus had written a very long math problem. "Oh no!" he thought to himself. "He must want me to answer that horrible-looking problem." Roland made a wild guess. "Fifty-four," he said.

"No!" replied Mr. Megalosaurus.

"Five hundred and two," said Roland, hopefully.

"NO!" said Mr. Megalosaurus, in a voice that made Roland quake.

"Three hundred and eight?" said Roland, in a very small voice.

Mr. Megalosaurus sighed. "I said it's time to go home, you *silly* dinosaur!"

Roland looked around him, and saw that the classroom was deserted. "Oh, thank you, Mr. Megalosaurus!" he said, and hurried off home!

The dinosaurs were having a picnic in the park. The sun was shining and there was lots to eat. When everyone had eaten their fill, and the adults lay down sleepily in the sun, Barry said, "Let's play on the slide!"

The children ran off toward the slide, but when Daisy set eyes on it, she began to cry.

"Whatever's the matter, Daisy?" burped Big Morton Megalosaurus when he saw her tears.

"Someone has broken the slide. I was having such a wonderful day, and now it's spoiled."

"Cheer up Daisy," grinned Morton. "I've got an idea. Come over here and stand on my tail."

Puzzled, Daisy stepped on to Big Morton's tail. He suddenly ducked his head down, lifted his tail in the air, and Daisy slid all the way down his back! Daisy and Barry took turns on Morton's sliding tail all day long, and thought it was much more fun than the real slide.

"Oh, Morton, that was great fun," said Daisy. "You've saved the day!"

Neville Saltasaurus just loved taking baths. He liked to have bubbles spilling over the side of the tub, and animal-shaped soaps, and extraordinary bath toys. He could lie in the tub for hours. The only trouble was that Neville was really too big for the tub—he always had to dangle his tail over the edge where it would soon get cold.

One day, Neville was lying in the tub as usual, thinking hard about how he could manage to keep his tail warm and make his bathtimes really perfect. Suddenly, he heard his sister Mandy, shouting.

"Oh no!" she cried. "I'll never be able to knit! Look at this sweater—it's such an odd shape, and it's far too big!"

Neville had just had an idea . . . Leaping out of the tub with a great splash, he thundered downstairs, leaving wet footprints everywhere. "I'll have it!" he panted. Neville slipped the sweater over his tail. It was a perfect fit. Mandy smiled. Neville would never have a cold tail in the tub again!

Billy Brontosaurus loved to play soccer. But the other dinosaurs wouldn't let him play in their game.

"You are much too clumsy," groaned Freddy, whom Billy had knocked over with his tail.

"Your big feet make huge craters in the field," squeaked Dilly, scrambling out of an *enormous* footprint.

"Popwhoossh," hissed the ball when Billy accidentally trod on it.

"You can't play with us," they all said. "Go away!"

Billy nearly cried. He could only watch as the other dinosaurs played his favorite game. They scored lots of goals and were having a great time. Then, Freddy kicked the ball so hard it flew into a tree. Nobody could reach it. They jumped up and down and threw sticks at it, but still the ball was stuck.

Suddenly, with a plop and a bounce, the ball rolled on to the pitch again! Billy had stood on his back legs, reached up with his long neck, and plucked the ball from the tree!

"Hurrah for Billy!" shouted Dilly.

"You can play soccer with us any time," said Freddy.

Billy was very happy.

I wish we had a garden," sighed Jemima as she gazed out of the window. It was a hot day and she could see her friend Daniel Diplodocus pruning his roses next door, but Jemima's family didn't have a garden. They lived in a first-floor apartment.

"We could make a garden," said her dad.

"Could we really?" asked Jemima excitedly.

"Yes," said her dad. "I'll show you how."

So that afternoon Jemima and her dad bought some seeds. (Dad said garden cress were best for a small garden). They filled an old foil cooking tray with dirt and planted the seeds carefully. Then Jemima watered them. She wanted it to look like a real garden, so she arranged pebbles in a line to make a path and cut out a shiny circle of foil to make a pond.

Jemima put her garden on a sunny windowsill and watered it every day. By the end of two weeks, it was full of green sprigs as big as her little finger.

"Now comes the best part," said Jemima's dad.

"What's that?" asked Jemima.

"We harvest them," he replied, "and then we eat them!"

They ate Jemima's garden cress with buttery toast and hard-boiled eggs. It was delicious.

Cedric was desperate to join the circus. He had been practicing all his circus acts for weeks. On the day of the audition, Cedric was very nervous as he met the Circus Manager, but he bravely went into the ring and climbed the long ladder to the trapeze. It was no good. Cedric was just too scared of heights to make the jump.

Next, he showed the Manager his acrobatics. Poor Cedric! He couldn't even do a handstand. The Circus Manager sighed. "Why not try juggling?" he asked

Cedric *did* try, but he was hopeless! The balls went rolling all over the floor. By this time, quite a crowd had gathered to watch the spectacle. They thought it was one of the funniest sights they'd seen in a long time. When the Circus Manager heard the laughter, he suddenly had an idea . . .

"You will be a clown!" he cried.

And Cedric made one of the best circus clowns ever!

Brenda was watching Mommy clear out her closet. All the old clothes went in a pile to throw away, and this pile was getting bigger and bigger. Then Mommy found a red dress with bright yellow flowers. It used to be her favorite dress. Mommy tried to put it on but it was far too small. She couldn't bear to throw it away, so she wondered what she could do with it.

"I know!" said Mommy, excitedly. "I'll use the material to make you a lovely new dress."

"Yuk!" said Brenda. "I don't want it," and she ran into her room to play with her toys.

Later that afternoon, Mommy came into Brenda's room. "I know who'll appreciate my lovely dress now," said Mommy, smiling. And she held up two tiny little dresses which she had made that afternoon. They were just right for Brenda's favorite doll and teddybear.

Joey loved climbing. He could climb any tree, wall, or fence that he came across, no trouble at all.

One day, his brother Jasper went out to play football with his friends. Joey wanted to go too, but Jasper told him he was too young to play with his friends, and no good at football.

Joey secretly followed his brother to the football field, and hid behind a tree.

A few minutes after the game had started, Michael kicked the football over a garden wall. "What do we do now?" asked Jasper angrily. "We'll never get it back!"

"We could fly my new kite," said Bob. But again, within a few minutes the kite flew up into the air and got stuck in the branches of a tree.

"Oh no!" cried Jasper. "Now what are we going to do?"

Just then, Joey appeared from behind the tree. "I'll get them for you!"

Before the boys could answer, Joey was scaling the wall into the garden. A few seconds later, the football flew over the wall back into the field. Then Joey climbed up the tall tree and untangled the kite from the branches with one hand.

When he touched ground again safely, the boys cheered. "Looks like we'll have to take my kid brother with us every time we go out to play," smiled Jasper.

Christa was very excited about her birthday party as it was just a week away.

"What shall I wear?" she asked her mother, looking through her closet.

"You can wear this lovely white dress," said Mommy, "with your red ribbon."

But the dress had a dirty smudge on it, so Christa's mommy put the dress in the washing machine and went to find some detergent.

"She's forgotten my ribbon," thought Christa and put it into the machine with the dress.

Later that day when Mommy took out the dress it had turned bright PINK!

"My dress!" sobbed Christa. "I can't wear it and I don't want a party!" she cried.

"Don't worry," said Mommy comfortingly. "We can make it into a pink party!"

And all the invitations to Christa's party said, "Come to my pink party. Everyone must wear something pink!"

Daisy was very good at dancing. When she had learned every dance there was to know, she decided to think up her own.

She practiced all afternoon in the living room, moving to the music on her stereo. At last, Daisy's new dance was nearly ready.

"I just can't think of an exciting way to finish it," she said. "Perhaps my brother will have some ideas."

She opened Brad's bedroom door and stepped straight onto a marble. She skidded across the floor, hit the bed-post, and did a perfect somersault onto the bed.

"Are you all right, Daisy?" asked Brad. "That was quite a fall!"

"It wasn't a fall," said Daisy. "It was the perfect finale to my new dance!"

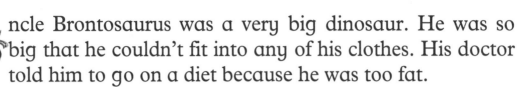

Uncle Brontosaurus was a very big dinosaur. He was so big that he couldn't fit into any of his clothes. His doctor told him to go on a diet because he was too fat.

Mommy made a special meal for all the family to help Uncle Brontosaurus get thin again. Rachel and Mark thought it was a horrid meal—just a few lettuce leaves and grapes.

"Have you had enough to eat?" asked Mommy.

"Yes, thank you," said Uncle Brontosaurus. "That was plenty for me."

After everyone had gone to bed, Mark began to get rather hungry . . .

He crept downstairs and into the kitchen. He found some cheese, and some slices of ham, and he made himself a very large sandwich. He was just about to take a bite, when he heard footsteps.

"A burglar!" he thought, and dived under the table. He could see the burglar's feet coming nearer, and finally, sitting down at the table!

"I'll get Daddy," he thought. As he crept out, he saw that the "burglar" was none other than Uncle Brontosaurus, and he was eating Mark's sandwich!

TIRED TOBY

Toby felt tired. It was a sunny, warm day, and his mom had given him a delicious hamburger for lunch. Now, all he wanted to do was amble down the garden to lie in a hollow and doze.

Meanwhile, a few streets away, Toby's friend, Brett, was busy in the front garden. He was helping his dad who had taken down an old fence and was wondering what to put up in its place.

"Shall we have a new ranch-style fence or a hedge?" asked Dad. "I can't make up my mind!"

Neither could Brett. "I'll go and ask Toby what he thinks," he said.

When Brett arrived at Toby's house, Toby's mom told him that Toby was fast asleep in the hollow at the bottom of the garden. All Brett could see of Toby was the row of big, bony plates that grew along his back.

"I know what dad should build," grinned Brett, hurrying home, "a craggy *stone wall*! Toby gave me the idea without even waking!"

Rex woke up with a start. It was very dark outside.

"Terry" he cried, "wake up!" Terry didn't stir. He was fast asleep.

"Wake up, Terry, please!" said Rex. "There's a giant dinosaur in the garden and I'm frightened."

Suddenly there was a bright flash of light and Terry sat up in bed with a start. "It's spitting fire!" he said.

They ran into their parents" room.

"Daddy, Daddy!" cried Terry. "There's a giant dinosaur in our garden, bigger than Uncle Brontosaurus and he's breathing fire and roaring!"

"Come with me," said Daddy.

He took Terry and Rex by the hand and led them to the window. Just then, the giant spat so much fire that it lit up the whole sky.

"That is lightning," said Daddy.

Then the giant roared so loudly that it made even Daddy jump.

"That is thunder," said Daddy.

Then it started to rain.

"It's not a monster," said Daddy. "Just a storm. You can go back to bed now." And Terry and Rex slept soundly all night.

ranny Tyrannosaurus was very old and rather forgetful. She had an enormous pair of false teeth, and she was always losing them.

One day, as usual, Granny Tyrannosaurus said, "I've lost my teeth."

Everyone sighed. "They should be easy to find," said Mommy—because they usually turned up somewhere.

The family began to search for Granny's teeth. Mommy looked in the kitchen in all the pots and pans; Frances looked in the pond, turning over the water lilies; Aunt Rose looked in the living room, checking under each pillow; Daddy simply looked everywhere he thought nobody else had looked; but nobody could find the teeth.

"Let's look again after lunch," said Mommy. "You must all be very tired."

"Yummy," said everyone at once, running into the kitchen. The search had made them very hungry.

Frances looked up with a mouthful of cake. "Oh Gran!" she said.

"Oh Gran!" said Aunt Rose.

"Oh Gran!" said Mommy. "You are silly. Your teeth are in your mouth!"

Daredevil Dinosaur worked at a film studio. He was especially trained to do stunt flying in all sorts of airplanes.

He appeared in lots of action-packed films and everyone called him Daredevil Dinosaur, although that wasn't his real name, of course.

One day, he visited his nephew, Neil, who loved to hear about his uncle's spectacular stunts.

"I'm sure there isn't a plane that you can't fly!" said Neil proudly.

"Not so far," replied Daredevil Dinosaur.

Then Neil showed him his model aircraft.

"I saved up and bought this," he said proudly.

Daredevil Dinosaur went to the park with Neil to try it out. Neil made the plane dip and twist in the air, then loop-the-loop.

When it was Daredevil Dinosaur's turn, the plane dived straight for him. Startled, he jumped out of the way just before the model crash-landed on the grass.

"Phew!" grinned Daredevil Dinosaur. "That's the first plane I *couldn't* fly!"

Mom, why have I such a long neck?" asked Neville.

"Some dinosaurs just do!" she smiled. "It can be very useful for looking into tall cupboards or peeping over folk's heads in a crowd," she went on. "You're lucky to have a long neck!"

"Am I?" sighed Neville, who was not at all sure about that, especially as he had nearly hit his head on the branch of a tree while walking home from school.

Neville's mom had an idea. The next day, she took Neville and his friend, Neil, to visit a maze.

"You two go in and enjoy yourselves," she said. "I'll sit here and rest!"

Neville and Neil followed some other visitors as they zigzagged to the middle of the maze. But no one knew the way out again. They were surrounded by tall hedges.

"What shall we do?" asked Neil.

"Follow me!" grinned Neville. He set off, turning this way and that, and soon arrived at the exit. Everyone cheered, including Neil.

"You're right, Mom!" called Neville happily. "Long necks are useful for getting out of trouble, too!"

"Mine!" shouted Rosie.

"Mine!" shouted Rex.

The terrible Tyrannosaurus twins were arguing over their toy truck. Rosie pulled it one way. Rex pulled it the other. The toy truck was about to break. . .

"If you don't let go," said Rex, "I'll dribble all over your dollhouse!"

"And if you don't let go," said Rosie, "I'll trample on your favorite teddy bear!"

"If you don't let go," shouted Rex, "I'll break your bike!"

"And if you don't let go," bellowed Rosie, "I'll kick your kite!"

"Well, if you don't let go," screamed Rex, "I'll bash up your bedroom!"

"If you don't let go," shrieked Rosie, "I'll stamp on your soldiers!"

"Well, if you two don't stop shouting," said Mrs. Tyrannosaurus, "there won't be any cake for lunch."

And you couldn't hear a squeak out of either of them.

FORGETFUL FRED

Fred lay in bed yawning. It was Monday. He hadn't done his homework. He couldn't be bothered to get up. He just knew it was going to be a rotten day.

"I don't want to go to school," his muffled voice told his mom from under the covers.

"Oh, you are so forgetful," she smiled.

His sisters peered around the door.

"You can't have forgotten," they giggled.

Fred could hear his father's deep, booming voice chuckling, "Fred forgetting his head again?"

Well, what if he did sometimes forget things. It wasn't fair to tease him. It was going to be a *very* rotten day. He rolled angrily out of bed, washed, and cleaned his teeth as slowly as he could, and then slouched grumpily into the kitchen for breakfast.

But what he found there soon changed his wrinkled frown to a huge grin.

"Happy Birthday, Fred!" cried his family, crowding around with cards, presents, and kisses, and pointing to a splendid cake on the table.

"Oh, Fred," said his mom, "You are so forgetful!"

Melissa had always wanted a garden of her own. She never forgot to water the seeds in her parents' garden, and was always first to spot the tiny, pale leaves pushing through the soil.

Today spring was in the air, and to Melissa's delight, when she asked if she could plant the seeds today, Mom said, "Yes, we'll plant them on the left of the path."

Melissa brought out the trowel and packet of seeds that Uncle Dip had given her for her birthday.

She dug the soil and pulled out the weeds—just as she had seen her mom do. Then she sifted the soil through some wire mesh until it was crumbly—just as she had seen her dad do. She made channels across the earth and sprinkled in her seeds, gently covering them over with her fingers. She watered the seeds and stuck a little marker in the earth with "Melissa's flowers" written on it. Just as she stood back to admire her work, Mom came into the garden.

Melissa pointed proudly at her handiwork. "Well," Mom gasped. "You are such a good gardener, you had better plant the other side of the path, too!"

And that spring, Melissa's flowers were the most beautiful in the whole garden.

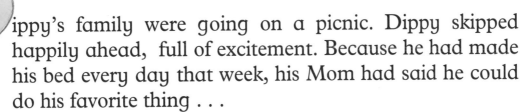

Dippy's family were going on a picnic. Dippy skipped happily ahead, full of excitement. Because he had made his bed every day that week, his Mom had said he could do his favorite thing . . .

As he rounded the bend, his twinkling green eyes saw the meadow and the pond, and beyond that, the brown, muddy swamp. With a yell of delight, he bounded off.

His family soon arrived. Mom and Dad settled down on the grass while the little ones played.

Suddenly, a mysterious glugging noise made them turn to the swamp. Great bubbles of mud were growing and bursting on the surface. Then a dome of mud rose from the murky swamp, and two twinkling green eyes blinked wickedly at them. They were frozen to the spot as they watched the shape grow. It was horrible! And it was coming toward them!

"Help! A monster!" the little ones shouted, as the large, brown, dripping beast advanced with a fearful roar.

Then the monster wiped its great paws across its face, smearing the mud from its green eyes and revealing the face of—Dippy!

"It's worth making my bed every day," he giggled, "if it means I can jump in the swamp!"

Mark couldn't sleep at night because he was so worried about not making friends at his new nursery.

When he arrived at the nursery, his mother gave him his lunchbox. "I don't want to go," he said, but his mother just smiled.

"You'll be all right," she told him.

Mark wandered in and met the other little dinosaurs. They all looked much more confident than he was. He drew pictures, listened to stories, and sang songs with his class, but he still felt too shy to talk to anyone. When lunchtime came, Mark opened his lunchbox. His mother had baked him some ginger cookies. She must have forgotten that Mark hated ginger more than anything else. The day was getting worse . . .

Just then, a pretty little, green-skinned dinosaur came up to him and said, "I'll give you my orange if you give me a cookie . . ."

Mark smiled and said, "OK!"

Soon, all the children were crowding around him, asking him for cookies. By the end of the day, he'd made friends with everyone in the class.

When Mark got home, he said, "Mom, can you bake some more ginger cookies? We all loved them!"

Alfred loved singing! He sang in the shower, in bed, on the bus, and especially in other people's houses. He thought his voice was beautiful, and even recorded some of his best songs on his tape deck. But everyone else thought he sounded awful.

"Stop screeching!" yelled his next door neighbor. The mailman dreaded delivering his mail, and his other neighbor permanently wore earplugs. But Alfred kept on singing!

Then a new family moved in down the road. They loved Alfred's singing. They asked him over for lots of parties, and always wanted him to sing afterward. They even borrowed his tape! Alfred felt much happier now that he had friends who liked his voice. With their encouragement he sang even more loudly and more often. Alfred thought his new friends were fantastic. But no one else did! I wonder why?

Dolly was learning to swim. She was jealous of her brother Darren when he plunged into the rippling water of the pond. And she was very angry with him when he leapt up and splashed her with cold spray.

"Go away," she cried. "I can swim if I need to."

"Not without your feet touching the bottom," he retorted, which was, in fact, almost true. No matter how hard she tried, Dolly could do only two or three strokes before her feet sank to the bottom.

"Today, I will swim," she said to herself in her most determined way, and splashed off for two-and-a-half strokes before her feet sank again.

Just then, a strong gust of wind blew across the pond. It lifted their clothes and towels on the bank—and blew Dolly's treasured cuddly dinosaur into the water!

"Toothy!" she cried, setting off at once across the water to rescue her beloved friend. Darren could not believe his eyes! Dolly was swimming—really swimming—without a single toe touching the bottom, all the way to Toothy, floating on the pond.

"Bravo!" he shouted as Dolly reached the sopping wet Toothy and dragged him to safety.

"I said I could swim if I needed to!" she said.

Mommy dreaded taking Robbie to the supermarket because he never behaved himself. As she pushed him around the aisles in a cart, he would knock things off the shelves, leaving a trail of frozen peas or grapes behind them. When Mommy wasn't looking, he would throw chocolates and cookies into the cart.

"What can I do with him?" Mommy thought in desperation. Then she noticed a little girl sitting quietly in a cart coloring some pictures in a coloring book.

Next time Mommy went shopping with Robbie she brought along some crayons and a coloring book. Robbie sat patiently coloring in the pictures of dinosaurs, and by the time he'd finished, they were home again.

Mom!" shouted Stephen, rushing home from school. "I'm in a play and I'm a king and I've got lines to say and a costume and you and Dad must come and it's for Christmas and I must learn my words and . . ."

"Goodness me, do take a breath," laughed Mom. Stephen couldn't wait to practice.

"Okay," said Mom. "I'll say Peter's line first . . . 'Who is this coming to visit the baby king?'"

"I am Balthasar and er . . . and . . ." said Stephen, forgetting the rest of the line.

"Beautifully spoken, dear," said his mom, "and the words were almost right. Let's try once more."

"I am Balthasar and I bring um . . . er . . ."

"We'll just keep practicing, shall we?" said his mom patiently. And that is what they did.

As the parents waited for the play to begin, no one was more anxious than Stephen's mom, for however hard he tried, he could not remember his words. As the kings strode on to the stage, she held her breath.

"Who is this coming to visit the baby king?" said Peter. Stephen stepped forward.

"I am Balthasar and I bring gold for the baby king," said Stephen. And his mom felt *very* proud.

Oliver Nodosaurus looked extremely fierce and had an enormously loud roar. Mrs. Protoceratops, the drama teacher, thought he would be perfect as the big bad monster in the school play.

Although Oliver did *look* very fierce, he was really very shy. He didn't want to be on stage one little bit, but he didn't dare refuse.

On the night of the school play, Oliver had terrible stage fright. He was too scared to go on stage and just stayed behind the curtains.

Just then, little Billy, who was sitting in the audience, saw Oliver's shadow fall across the stage floor. "Ooh look!" he shouted. "There's the monster! You can see his enormous shadow!"

The audience thought it was a very clever way to show the monster. It was much more frightening to see just the shadow, and imagine what the monster looked like, than to see an actor playing the part.

"The drama teacher must be *very* clever," they said. And nobody knew what had *really* happened except Oliver and Mrs. Protoceratops, who didn't mind a bit!

Bill and Betty stared through the window at the gray sky.

"We won't be able to go to the park today," Bill complained. "Look, it's starting to rain already. And I so wanted to play outside with my friends."

"Never mind, dear," said his dad. "You can play with your toys today, and perhaps it will be sunny tomorrow."

But they quickly tired of any games. They started to play with first one thing, then another, but they were always drawn back to the window, where the rain streamed down faster and faster by the minute.

"Look at those raindrops," said Betty gloomily. "The harder it rains, the faster they go . . . That's it! We can play races with the raindrops."

In minutes they were utterly absorbed, squeaking and roaring with excitement as first one raindrop, then another cascaded down the window and dashed across the finishing line!

And who won all the races at the end of the day? The dinosaurs were enjoying themselves so much, they forgot to count!

Dickon loved playing among the plants at the end of his garden. When he was on his own, he liked nothing better than tracking minibeasts. Crouching down with his nose pressed to the ground, he would follow the tiny creatures, tracking their every move.

One day, he spotted a big caterpillar. Dickon had never seen such a wonderful creature and he watched, fascinated, as it devoured chunks out of a leaf.

For days Dickon tracked his caterpillar. He only had to follow the trail of nibbled leaves and he was sure to find it. Until one day there was nothing—nothing except a fat brown lump of a thing hanging from a stem. Dickon shuffled off to find his friends. Minibeast tracking did not seem the same any more.

Some time later, Dickon again came across the fat brown lump of a thing. He gently touched it with his nose. It made a papery, cracking sound, then it slowly split and a slender creature appeared. The crumpled paper on its back stretched out, and before Dickon's astonished eyes, there was a beautiful butterfly. It lifted into the air, circled once as if to say goodbye, then flew away. Dickon's caterpillar had become a butterfly.

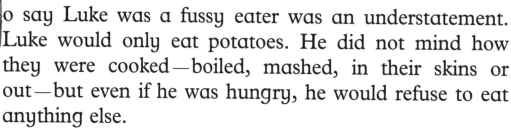

To say Luke was a fussy eater was an understatement. Luke would only eat potatoes. He did not mind how they were cooked—boiled, mashed, in their skins or out—but even if he was hungry, he would refuse to eat anything else.

"I'm sure there are more things you like than just potatoes!" his mom complained.

Mom was planning the games for Luke's birthday party. Luke loved playing games, especially the surprise games his mom always invented. This year, she planned to surprise him more than usual.

"This game is 'Test your Taste'," she announced to the excited children. "Put on your blindfolds, then taste the food in bowls and see if you can guess what it is."

The little dinosaurs poked around with their spoons, managing to smear almost as much food on each other's faces as they got into their mouths! Finally the food-spattered papers were handed in. For every single one, Luke had written, "Potatoes!"

"I liked them all," he explained with a grin, "so I thought they must all be potatoes."

"Not one of them was potatoes," laughed Mom, "so tomorrow you can have something else for lunch!"

MONTY'S SUNGLASSES

Monty's sunglasses wouldn't stay on his nose. He bought a red round pair, then a blue star-shaped pair, and an orange triangle pair, but they all kept slipping off.

"I have to wear sunglasses or the sun hurts my eyes," Monty complained, but he couldn't find a pair to fit.

When Monty went to the beach with his friends he had to sit in the shade because it was a very sunny day.

"Come and play on the beach," called his friends, but Monty stayed under a tree. Then his best friend Oliver came back from the stores with some ice cream and a special present for Monty . . .

"Try this on," he said, and gave Monty a bright red baseball cap. It fitted perfectly, shading his eyes from the sun. Monty was delighted and ran to join his friends playing football on the beach.

Richard was working for his cook's badge at Dinocubs. He had learned to make scrambled eggs on toast, and a fruit and nut salad. Uncle Charlie said his stew and dumplings were "quite passable'—and he should know because he ate enough of them.

But what Richard liked making best were rock cakes—crunchy outside and soft inside, with juicy raisins in each mouthful. Richard had to bake the cakes at the next Dinocubs meeting. He measured out the ingredients, but Mom could not find any large enough pans.

"I know," said Mom, "just make half the recipe."

Richard set off, confident that his cook's badge was as good as won. With the flair of an expert chef, he tossed in flour and butter, fruit and egg. The mixture did seem sloppier than usual, but never mind.

Ping! Time to get them out. But what a shock! Instead of crunchy rock cakes, all he could see were soft and rounded pale mud cakes. Richard hung his head. What about his badge now? Dinoleader said nothing. When they were cool, he took a bite.

"These mud cakes are as tasty as your rock cakes," he said. "You have earned your badge." He realized what Richard and his Mom had not. When they halved the recipe, they forgot to add only half the egg!

Leyla was looking for her pens and pencils. She had searched everywhere.

"If you put things away, you would know where to find them again," said her mom, taking the pencils from the box and handing them to Leyla.

"Have you seen my yo-yo, Mom?" asked Lucy, coming into the kitchen. Mom reached into a toy box and handed it to her.

"If you put it away, you would know where to find it again," said Mom.

When it was time to do the shopping, Mom began to rush about the rooms, looking here and there, in pockets and on chairs.

"Has anyone seen my keys?" she asked. The little ones started to help, lifting pillows and opening drawers until, at last, the keys were found, hidden under a hat on the table.

The dinosaurs resisted the temptation to say anything, but Mom laughed.

"I know," she said. "If I put them away, I would know where to find them again!"

Doreen's neighbors were painting the outside of their house. Doreen loved painting. "Can I help?" she asked.

"All right, if you're very careful," said the neighbors.

They had red paint for the walls, and white paint for the window frames. Doreen went around to the back of the house, away from everyone else, where she had a whole wall to herself. She painted a big umbrella, and a beachball, and a dinosaur in a red and white striped swimsuit. She had a wonderful time.

Then she heard a friend of the neighbors arrive, who had come to visit them. They all walked around the house, and suddenly saw the wall Doreen had been painting. The neighbors were very angry, but just as they opened their mouths to say something, their friend exclaimed, "How clever! A sunny beach scene to look at all year round! Would you do one for me?"

The neighbors liked the idea of starting a new fashion. Suddenly, they began to smile. Doreen was very relieved, and spent the whole summer painting houses!

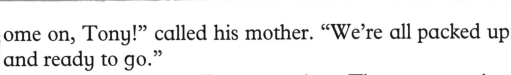

Come on, Tony!" called his mother. "We're all packed up and ready to go."

The family was off on vacation. They were going camping by the beach, and they were taking so many things. Buckets and spades, sleeping bags, pots and pans, books and games, and T-shirts and shorts.

"I'm not going without Steggy," said Tony, crossly. Steggy was the toy Stegosaurus who had shared Tony's bed since he was tiny. He couldn't go to sleep without Steggy, and now he had lost him.

"We're not waiting any longer, Tony," said his father. "You're coming—NOW!"

So Tony came, but he wasn't happy. He grumbled and moaned all the way to the beach. And when it was time to go to bed in their cozy tent, he just cried.

"Cheer up, Tony," said his sister, unrolling his sleeping bag for him. And who should fall out but—Steggy!

"I remember now," said Tony happily, "I packed him myself, so he wouldn't be forgotten. Now I'm going to have the best vacation ever!"

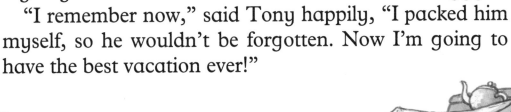

Rachel had seen a poster for a circus. It showed acrobats and tightrope walkers, performing dogs and clowns.

"I'm sorry, but it's too far for us to go," said her dad. Rachel was very disappointed, and told her friend Chuck all about it.

"Let's make our own circus, instead," he suggested. "We could do anything we like. I bet our friends would come to watch—and they could join in, too!" So all that afternoon they practiced their acts, until they were ready with a splendid show.

Chuck did cartwheels and somersaults—forward and backward—and balanced on a plank of wood. Rachel danced and stood on one leg on the swing—and everyone pretended that she was very high off the ground. They tossed hoops to each other, then put on silly hats and chased around the ring. It was such a marvelous circus, that the audience even joined in for the grand parade, marching around and pretending to play musical instruments. And none of them even gave a thought to the other circus—they were all having too much fun.

Jeanette and Jessica were identical twins. Both had the same green eyes, the same brown, scaly skin, the same long tails. Only dinosaurs who knew them well had learned to tell them apart. One day, Murray was boasting that he was the fastest runner in school.

"I'm fed up with him showing off," said Jessica. "I have an idea to teach him a lesson."

The next day, the twins and their friends were having races in the playground. Up marched Murray.

"Slowpokes," mocked Murray. "I can run twice as fast as that without even trying!" Jeanette came forward while Jessica quietly walked away, unnoticed.

"Race you around the school then," challenged Jeanette.

"I'm ready any time," said Murray. Timmy was to be the starter. Jeanette and Murray lined up.

"On your marks, get set—go!" said Timmy, and they raced off around the school.

Murray slowly took the lead, but Jeanette was close behind as they raced past the tree where Jessica had hidden. Jeanette slipped into the hiding place, as Jessica dashed out, so full of energy that she soon overtook Murray and beat him to the finishing line. Everyone cheered the winner—and Murray never found out that he was only beaten by twin speed!

It's not fair," moaned Rebecca. "I want a day off school like Scott."

"Scott has spots, a high temperature, and doesn't feel well," said Mom. "You'll have more fun at school than he will at home."

Rebecca went off to school in a bad mood. She could not concentrate on her lessons because she kept thinking about Scott at home. She imagined he was having a great time while she was hard at work. It wasn't fair! She did not know that while she was building a cardboard spaceship, listening to stories, measuring the desks, and rushing about the playground, Scott was in bed feeling hot, itchy, and unhappy.

When Rebecca woke up the next morning, she felt hot and itchy. Her face was pink and blotchy and she could not eat her breakfast.

"Back to bed," ordered Mom.

"But Mrs. Bronto said we could paint pictures of our garden today and we are going on a nature walk," wailed Rebecca, almost in tears. "It's not fair." Her Mom smiled kindly as she tucked her back into bed.

"This time, I agree with you," she said. "It's not nice feeling sick—as I am sure Scott could have told you yesterday. It's much more fun at school."

CHOCOLATE ECLAIRS

Jessie was a very lucky dinosaur. Her grandma owned a bakery, and every day her mom would take her there and let her play while she helped Grandma bake cakes. The bakery was full of delicious things, like ice cream and cinnamon rolls. But the things that Jessie liked best were the chocolate éclairs. One day, the telephone rang while Grandma was making the chocolate frosting for the éclairs. She went off to answer it, leaving the bowl on the table. Jessie knew she would get into trouble if her grandma found her licking the bowl, so as quick as a flash, she took the whole thing and ran off into the garden. The chocolate frosting was delicious! Jessie ate spoon after spoon.

Inside, she heard Grandma saying, "I'm sure I left some frosting just there. I must be going crazy!"

Jessie laughed and laughed, but suddenly, she began to feel very ill . . .

Betsy's father loved gardening. He spent every weekend pulling out the weeds and trimming the lawn. He was very proud of all his work, and his was the best-kept garden in the neighborhood. He had a big vegetable patch at the back of the garden where he grew potatoes, rhubarb, and cabbages. This year he was planning to enter some of his potato plants in the local gardening competition, and had spent more time than ever tending to them, until the plants stood even taller than Betsy!

One day, Betsy and her friend Dinah were playing in the garden. One of their favorite games was making houses, and the big potato plants looked a perfect place for a cozy little house. They walked in, pushed the big leafy plants aside, until they got right to the middle. Then they squashed down all the leaves into a circle. It was a perfect house! It was cool and green and had a path all the way out to . . . Oops! There, at the end of the path, stood Betsy's dad. And he didn't look very happy!

THE NEST

All Katie's friends seemed to have lots of brothers and sisters. Sometimes, Katie thought it was better to have her mom and dad to herself. But at other times, she wished she was part of a large brood so she always had someone to play with.

Early one spring, her mother seemed preoccupied and was often too tired to play with Katie. At other times she bustled about looking very busy, although Katie could never quite work out what she was doing. Dad was too busy decorating to spare her any time. Katie felt lonely and left out.

One day, she came home late from a walk. She had been daydreaming about belonging to a big family and had forgotten the time. She rushed into the room, her excuse ready, expecting to be told off. But her mother just rushed up to her and gave her a hug! Then she led Katie into the newly decorated room.

Katie could hardly believe her eyes. There in the corner, tucked up soft and cozy, was a nest. And inside the nest were four beautiful, green eggs.

"You are going to have some brothers and sisters soon," said her mom proudly. "Will you help me to care for them?"

"Oh, yes," cried Katie. "I'll be the best big sister ever."

Dan was having trouble with his arithmetic at school.

"I always get the numbers mixed up," he said grumpily, stamping his foot, as he often did when he was angry. "I'm not going to do any more. I don't care if I can't remember."

His Mom knew better than to argue with him when he was feeling so angry. She watched him run down the path to his favorite thinking place—the gate at the bottom of the garden. He always sat there when he wanted to sulk, she thought to herself. Then an idea came to her, and she got out a pencil and paper and jotted down a little rhyme to help Dan with his addition.

"Pat a cake, pat a cake
Stamp on the floor
Two plus two is always four!
Pat a cake, pat a cake
Sit on the gate
Four plus four is always eight!"

And even though Dan is much bigger now, he always remembers that little rhyme.

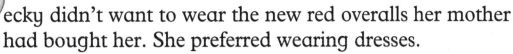

Becky didn't want to wear the new red overalls her mother had bought her. She preferred wearing dresses.

"But you must wear them," pleaded her mother. "You'll look so sweet—and they're your favorite color."

When it was time to go to the park, Becky was still upstairs in her bedroom, dressed in her pajamas.

"We'll go without you!" threatened her mother. Becky reluctantly put on her new overalls.

At the park, Becky soon found she could join all the other dinosaurs climbing up the steep steps of the long slide, playing on the seesaw, and sitting in the sandbox, without her dress getting in the way as it usually did.

"I like my new overalls!" said Becky happily, when her mother took her home.

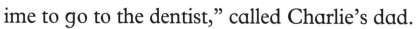

T ime to go to the dentist," called Charlie's dad.

"I don't want to!" shouted Charlie. He was hiding.

"If you don't go to the dentist," said Mr. Centro-saurus pulling Charlie out of his hiding place, "you'll never grow up with big strong, healthy teeth."

"Noooo!" cried Charlie all the way to the dentist.

"Waaaaah!" he wailed in the dentist's waiting room.

"What bad manners," whispered a lady patient.

Charlie's dad let go of him. Charlie ran through a door and found himself in a big white room. In the middle of the room was a shiny silver chair with levers on it. Charlie sat in the chair and pulled some of the levers. The chair whizzed up and down.

"Are you Charlie?" said a voice. "What lovely teeth. Can I see them?" It was a lady in a white coat.

"All right," said Charlie. "I've just escaped from the dentist," he added proudly.

The lady whizzed him up on the chair and looked at his teeth with a little mirror. Then she polished them with a special electric brush.

"All done," she said. "That wasn't so bad, was it?"

"No," said Charlie. "That was fun!"

Then Charlie's dad appeared at the door and Charlie realized . . . he had been at the dentist's all along!

I'm not scared of anything!" boasted Susie Stegosaurus.

"Well, I bet you don't dare go into the haunted house," sneered her brother, James.

"Bet you don't, either," said Susie.

"Bet I do, too," said James. "Let's go right now."

Susie and James sneaked up the overgrown path and pushed open the creaky door.

"I'm not s-scared," shivered Susie.

"M-me neither," trembled James.

They crept up the winding stairs.

"Bet you're f-frightened," stammered James.

"I'm n-no scaredycat," stuttered Susie.

They opened the door of the dark, cobwebby room and tiptoed in.

"W-well," whispered Susie, "I suppose neither of us are scaredycats."

"I s-suppose not," whispered James.

"Eeeeek!" squeaked a mouse.

"Arrrghhh!" screamed James.

"Help!" shrieked Susie.

And they both ran out of the cobwebby room and down the winding stairs, through the creaky door, and up the overgrown path, all the way back home to bed.

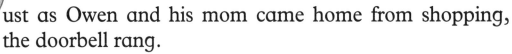

Just as Owen and his mom came home from shopping, the doorbell rang.

"I wanted to catch you before you took off your coat," Mrs. Dimetrodon said as they opened the door. "Please tell me the name of these lovely blue flowers."

"I won't be long, Owen," Mom sighed as she was led next door. Suddenly, a gust of wind blew the door closed with a bang.

"Oh!" cried Mom. "My keys are in the house. Owen," she called. "Can you open the door?" But Owen was too small to reach the latch.

"Get a chair," said Mom. But the latch was too stiff for Owen's small hands.

"I'm locked in," wailed Owen. "I want my mom!"

"What shall we do?" muttered the little crowd which was by now spreading down the path.

Mom pulled out a hanky to blow her nose, because she was beginning to feel upset. There was a loud jingle in her pocket and all the chattering stopped.

"Oh dear!" said Mom, holding up the keys and blushing. "They must have been there all the time."

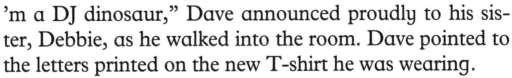

I'm a DJ dinosaur," Dave announced proudly to his sister, Debbie, as he walked into the room. Dave pointed to the letters printed on the new T-shirt he was wearing.

"What does that mean?" asked Debbie, who was much more interested in a colorful box she had bought.

"Disc jockey!" replied Dave. "My friend, Mike, has asked me to pick and play the music at his party tomorrow. His mom even gave me this special T-shirt from the clothes store she owns."

While Dave sorted through his collection of tapes, Debbie placed her box on the table. When Dave turned around, she asked him to open it.

As her brother lifted the lid, a funny toy insect sprang out and squeaked loudly. It made Dave jump!

"I bought that from the joke store!" giggled Debbie.

"I'm going to ask Mike if his mom has another 'DJ' T-shirt for you," Dave laughed.

"Why? I'm not a disc jockey," said his sister.

"No," grinned Dave. "You're *Debbie* the *Joker*!"

Dad was going to take Billy and his friend Trevor to the park, but first they had to clean up the house. Billy helped Dad to do the dishes.

"No, Billy. Not like that—like this," said his father, rinsing all the suds off the dishes.

Then there were lots of Billy's clothes to put away.

"No, Billy. Not like that—like this," said Dad, folding them up neatly.

Then all the toys had to be put away.

"No, Billy. Not like that—like this," said Dad, finding the right box for each one.

At last it was time to go. When they got to the park, Dad started to play football. He was hopeless!

"No, Dad. Not like that—like this," said Billy, kicking the ball for a field goal. Then Trevor got his skateboard out. Dad wanted a turn riding it.

"No, not like that—like this," said Trevor, showing him how to balance.

Then they played tag. Billy caught Dad every time.

"Your dad's not much good at playing," said Trevor.

"I know," said Billy. "But he's learning."

O h, Mom!" wailed Jack, looking out of the window. "It's raining hadrosaurs and stegosaurs!'

Jack's friend Catherine was coming to play, and Mom had promised them a picnic in the park. But how could they have a picnic in the pouring rain?

"Never mind," said Mom. "I've got an idea." She took a big tablecloth out of the drawer and went into the kitchen, shutting the door behind her.

When Catherine arrived, she and Jack played cards for a while. When Mom called out, "Time to eat!" they raced into the kitchen.

In the middle of the floor was their very own dinosaur den, with the table for a roof and the tablecloth for walls—and the picnic was ready and waiting for them inside! Mom had piled rocks all around, and there was a big sign pinned to the cloth that said "Jack and Catherine's cave—keep out!"

"Oh, Mom," said Jack, "this is great! Can we always have our picnics inside?"

John had a very tiny dinosaur friend. He was called Rocky. Rocky was a little shy, and spent a lot of his time sleeping. He liked nothing better than to curl up in John's mom's warm ironing basket, on top of all the clothes.

One day, John lost Rocky. He looked in the ironing basket, but there was nothing there. He looked all over his room, under the bed, and behind the bookcase. He even looked in the rock garden outside, where Rocky liked to play at being a big ferocious dinosaur in the plants and stones. But Rocky wasn't there either.

Just then, John heard some tiny squeaking noises that seemed to be coming from his chest of drawers. Then he heard the noise again. He walked up to the top drawer very carefully, and opened it quickly. There was Rocky, looking rumpled and a bit annoyed! He had fallen asleep in the ironing, and been put away in the drawer along with the rest of the clothes. Poor Rocky! John was very pleased to have found him again.

Your cousin Lorraine's coming to stay next week," Mom said to Sarah. "That'll be nice, won't it?"

"No," said Sarah. She remembered when Lorraine had come to stay last year. She'd brought lots of dolls and all she did was sit inside and play with them. She always looked neat and tidy, and everyone said, "What a good little dinosaur Lorraine is!"

But Lorraine was different this time. She didn't bring any dolls with her—she brought a scooter. And she certainly didn't look neat and tidy!

On Monday, Lorraine made a den out of chairs and a rug in the living room.

On Tuesday, Lorraine dug up all the flowers in the garden to make a big bonfire.

On Wednesday, Lorraine crashed her scooter into Mrs. Iguanadon's fence.

On Thursday, Lorraine made a very strange cake—using all the food in the cupboard.

On Friday, Lorraine and Sarah had a midnight feast.

On Saturday, it was time for Lorraine to go home.

"Can Cousin Lorraine come and stay again soon?" asked Sarah.

"No," said her mother. "Let's have a rest from Lorraine for a while."

Charlie loved bicycles. Every day, on the way to school, he would stop and gaze in the window of the bicycle store. There were all sorts of bicycles, but Charlie liked one special shiny red one. He asked his parents if they would buy it for him, but they just said, "Don't be silly. You can't even *ride* a bicycle!"

Charlie's friend Gary was an acrobat in the circus, and was very good at balancing on things. "Would you help me learn to ride a bicycle?" Charlie asked.

Gary helped Charlie practice. It was very difficult and Charlie kept falling off. But eventually he could stay on with Gary holding him. Finally, Gary let go! Charlie wobbled a bit, but rode all the way home with Gary running along behind. His parents were amazed to see him riding up the driveway all by himself!

The next morning, when Charlie opened his eyes, he saw a beautiful red shiny bicycle right next to his bed!

THE BIRTHDAY PRESENT

William and Joanna were in a fix. Mom's birthday was in two days but they could not think of anything nice that they could afford to buy. Dad was not much help.

"She won't expect you to buy a present," he said. "Why not paint her a picture instead?" But they wanted to buy her a present. So they sat in their thinking spot in the garden and vowed to stay there until they had a plan. It took until lunchtime before William had an idea.

The next day, they returned from the stores, hiding a brown paper bag behind their backs. Paper and paints were sneaked into their bedroom where laughter could be heard through the closed door.

The next morning, Mom was woken at just the right time with a cup of tea, a beautifully painted birthday card, and a chorus of "Happy Birthday!"

"Thank you," replied Mom, admiring the colorful flowers on the card. "Is that me wearing the knitted hat? It suits me. And the flowers are lovely."

"Oh, good," the little dinosaurs replied, handing her a brown paper package painted with flowers. Mom opened it to reveal a packet of seeds and some yarn. "We bought you the seeds and the yarn, and the pictures are to show what they will look like when you have grown the flowers and knitted the hat."

"What a clever idea," said Mom.

THE WISHING POOL

One sunny day, a young dinosaur named Morris was sitting beside a pool, dreaming about this and that and watching the other dinosaurs in the forest.

"I wish I had three fine horns like Triceratops," he thought to himself. At once, he felt a strange tingling in his head. And when he looked at himself in the still water, there were the horns!

"This must be a wishing pool!" thought Morris. And in no time at all he had wished for wings like Pteranodon, a long neck like Diplodocus, and teeth like Tyrannosaurus Rex.

"Help! It's a monster!" screamed his mother when Morris came home for lunch, flapping his wings, stretching his neck, and baring his teeth.

"Go away!" shouted Morris's friends when he tried to play with them.

"Grrrr!" growled the great Tyrannosaurus when he saw Morris's sharp teeth.

Morris went straight back to the pool and wished as hard as he could to be ordinary Morris. After that, he never tried wishing again!

Terry and Rex were on their way to see Auntie Dinah and her new baby. They were very excited at the thought of a new playmate.

"Where is it?" cried Terry when they arrived.

"There," said Auntie Dinah, pointing to a smooth shiny object in the corner. "It's in the egg."

It didn't move or smile or play. "Babies are boring," said Terry and went out to play.

Rex was reading a book when he heard a sound. "CRACK" it went, and "CRACK" again, and then, "CRACK." Rex saw a little hole appear in the egg. It got bigger and bigger. Out popped a head and then a body. And there, looking curiously at him, was the cutest little dinosaur in the world.

"Terry, Terry! Come and see!" yelled Rex.

Terry rushed in. "Oh wow!" he said. "Babies aren't boring after all!"

I was a fine day so Big Dinosaur and Little Dinosaur put on their sun hats and took a picnic to the beach.

"Perhaps we should have gone to the park instead," said Little Dinosaur shortly after they arrived.

"Why?" asked Big Dinosaur.

"There are lots of shady trees to sit under," replied Little Dinosaur. "I'm getting hot!"

Big Dinosaur went to the beach store to rent a large umbrella but they were all being used.

"One's due to be returned very soon," said the store owner. "Then you can have it."

"What shall we do until then?" asked Little Dinosaur when he heard.

"I'll show you some shade," grinned Big Dinosaur.

Little Dinosaur was puzzled. All he could see was hot sand. "Where?" he asked.

Big Dinosaur lay on his towel and pulled the sun hat over his eyes. Little Dinosaur laughed. "Now I see the shade!" he said. "I can sit in your huge *shadow*!"

Karl's dad took him to a fairground. But, try as he might, Karl could not win a prize at the Toss the Ring stall.

"Watch me, son," grinned Dad.

Taking aim, he tossed a hoop over a jar of cookies and won them! On the way home, Karl thoughtfully munched a cookie. "I really enjoyed myself. Thanks, Dad," he said. "I wish I could throw a hoop like you did!"

"It just takes practice," Dad replied. "I'll help you, if you like."

Karl eagerly agreed, so his dad found some small rubber rings in the garage. Then he called Karl.

"All you have to do is throw the rings at me," said Dad. Karl was puzzled.

"How will playing catch help?" he asked.

His dad chuckled. "Not catch, silly. Toss the Ring! You have to toss the hoops over my horns."

Karl carefully began to toss the rings over the three horns on his dad's head. Soon he could do it with ease. And next day, when they returned to the Toss the Ring stall, who do you think won a prize? Karl, of course!

Mr. Diplodocus was a very stylish dresser. There wasn't a single day that he wasn't well dressed, all the long way from his top hat to his shiny shoes.

But what Mr. Diplodocus wanted more than anything else, was a bow tie. Luckily, it was his birthday in one week's time, so it was a perfect opportunity to tell all his friends what he wanted. And that is exactly what he did.

On his birthday, Mr. Diplodocus had *piles* of presents. He unwrapped the first present, and was delighted to find a pink and blue striped bow tie. "Wonderful!" he exclaimed, and went on to unwrap the second gift. "Another bow tie!" he cried. And so it went on. Every single package contained a colorful bow tie.

Luckily for Mr. Diplodocus, he didn't have to upset any of his friends by wearing only one of his presents — he had such a long neck that he could wear every single one. What a spectacular sight Mr. Diplodocus made, as he walked proudly down the street wearing no less than twenty bow ties!

Sam loved chocolate more than anything else.

"One of these days you'll turn into chocolate," his mom warned. That night, Sam sat in bed reading a book about a chocolate tree. Soon he fell asleep.

Sam could see the chocolate tree in front of him as he walked through the forest. As he got nearer, he thought he could make out a gnarled face in the folds of the bark. Suddenly, a broad smile spread across the tree and two beady eyes popped open.

"Hello," said a deep, chocolaty voice. "Do take a bite." Sam picked off a few leaves. They melted on his tongue. He couldn't resist just another bite—or two, or three. Then his hands felt sticky. He tried to wipe them clean on his handkerchief, but to his dismay, he found that he could not wipe the chocolate off his fingers, for his fingers *were* chocolate—and his arms, and his legs!

"But I don't want to be chocolate!" he cried out.

"I was only joking, dear," said his mom. "You won't turn into chocolate." Sam opened his eyes.

"I do like chocolate, Mom," he said. "But I think I'll eat less of it from now on."

Ben was bored. He'd been playing by himself all morning and now he'd run out of things to do.

"Come outside," called his mother. "It's a beautiful spring day and you can help me with the gardening."

"Gardening's boring," said Ben.

"No, it's not," said his mother. "Look, you can have this patch of earth and make a garden all your own."

"All right," said Ben. He found the shells he'd picked up on the beach last summer and put them all around the edge. His mother gave him some seeds, and he dug a tiny hole for each one with a teaspoon, popped it in and covered it up with earth. He sprayed the seeds with water so they would grow.

Then one fine summer's day, Ben was running down the path when he saw a jungle of nasturtiums, cornflowers, and marigolds.

"Look, I grew these flowers," said Ben to his mother. "Gardening's great!"

Terence Pterodactyl was an extremely clever little dinosaur. At school he did well in every subject. There was nothing that Terence Pterodactyl couldn't do.

One day, his teacher announced to the class that she was going to give them a spelling test. All Terence's friends were very worried about it. But not Terence—he could spell anything, no trouble at all.

At the spelling test, the teacher said, "Emma—spell JURASSIC."

"J-E-R-A-S-S-I-K," said Emma, nervously,

"That's wrong," said the teacher. "Terence—*you* try."

"J-U-R-A-S-S-I-C," he quickly replied.

"Well done, Terence. You *are* clever," said the teacher. "Now spell PTERODACTYL."

"Easy!" he sneered. But try as he might, Terence couldn't get it right. The word *seemed* to begin with a "T," it *sounded* like a "T," and yet every time he started off with "T," the teacher shouted "Wrong!" Poor Terence didn't know it started with a "P."

His friends suddenly felt much better—Terence, the dinosaur who could do anything, couldn't spell his own name! "Never mind, Terry," they said, after school. "At least you know what it feels like to be wrong!"

Daisy had a parasol which she carried everywhere. Sunny or cloudy, whatever the weather, she never left it behind. One dull day, Daisy walked around the garden happily twirling the parasol over her head.

"Why carry that silly parasol when the sun isn't shining?" teased her brother, Brad. "I'm off next door, to play marbles with Mark. Want to join us?"

Daisy shook her head. She wanted to play with her parasol. She was still in the garden when her mom called, "Lunchtime! Go and get Brad, please!"

Mark and Brad were putting away their marbles. Suddenly, her brother's bag split. All the marbles dropped out and rolled across the floor.

"How will I get them home?" said Brad as he began to pick them up.

"Easy," smiled Daisy. Opening her parasol, she held it upside-down like a basket and put the marbles into it.

"Parasols aren't so silly!" admitted Brad. "Shall *I* carry it home for you, Daisy?"

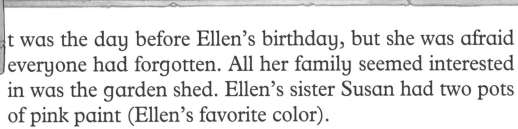

It was the day before Ellen's birthday, but she was afraid everyone had forgotten. All her family seemed interested in was the garden shed. Ellen's sister Susan had two pots of pink paint (Ellen's favorite color).

"I'm going to paint the shed," said Susan, "so it will look pretty this summer."

When Ellen's mom came in that evening, she had a big bag of ribbons and silver paper.

"I'm going to decorate the shed," said Ellen's mom, "so it will look cheerful this summer."

Grandpa was hiding something behind his back.

"I'm putting these pillows in the shed," he said, "so we can sit there when it's warm."

Ellen's brother, Tom, had some lemonade and cakes.

"I suppose they're for the shed, too," sighed Ellen.

"Yes," he said. "I'm going to store them in there."

On Ellen's birthday there were no cards, no decorations, and no cake. They *had* forgotten.

"Come and see the shed, Ellen," said her family.

When Ellen opened the shed door her family shouted "SURPRISE!" The shed was painted pink with HAPPY BIRTHDAY ELLEN on the wall in silver paper, and on the table were cards, presents, and a great big birthday cake. They *had* remembered after all.

Naomi was a very pretty dinosaur with beautiful, crinkly, green skin and a cute little horn on her pointed snout. The trouble was that Naomi was proud of being pretty, and she let everyone know it!

One day, the class was taking a boat trip. They set off in a neat line of pairs, but Naomi walked alone.

"None of you is good-looking enough to walk with me," she said, lifting her snout higher into the air.

With their coats buttoned tight and the wind on their scales, they pointed over stern and bow, chattering incessantly, as the Captain pointed out the sights. Naomi sat alone, not happy at being ignored.

Suddenly, it began to rain, and all the dinosaurs rushed quickly toward the cabin. All except Naomi, who ambled after them, snout so high that she did not see the rope across the deck and fell headlong into a puddle. The children laughed when they saw her bedraggled pink bow and muddy face. For once, Naomi was not happy to be the center of attention.

"No one likes me," she wailed to Mrs. Skeggs.

"Why not try liking them?" suggested Mrs. Skeggs. "Then perhaps they will like you, too."

Naomi dried her tears, straightened her bow and smiled. "I'll try," she said. And she did.

R ight on time!" grinned Mr. Docus as Mark opened the gate and hurried up the path to the front door with the "Dinosaur News." Mark always arrived at five o'clock each afternoon, on his paper route.

Next morning, a cement-mixer rumbled in Mr. Docus's front yard as he started to lay a new path.

He finished just minutes before Mark was due with the newspaper. Mr. Docus went indoors and wrote "WET CEMENT" on some cardboard to tie to the gate.

Mrs. Docus peered from the window at the cement path. "It's very plain," she said. "It needs a pattern."

"What sort?" asked Mr. Docus, thinking hard. He forgot about Mark, who came racing up the path as usual, leaving a perfect trail of footprints behind him.

"I'm sorry!" he said when he saw what he had done.

"Don't be," laughed Mr. Docus. "It's the perfect path pattern!"

"And most unusual," Mrs. Docus agreed.

Emma was a shy dinosaur. She loved to play with dolls and read books. She had lots of friends, but what she wanted most of all was a special friend of her own.

One day, their teacher introduced them to Sally, who was joining the class. Hands shot into the air.

"Can I look after her?" "Oh, me!" cried the children. But Emma was too shy to put up her hand.

Kitty and Michael were chosen, and for the first week, they showed Sally where everything was kept and played with her at playtime and lunchtime. Emma just watched. She very much wanted to be Sally's friend, too, but she was too shy to say anything.

Sally soon settled into the class and Kitty and Michael began to play with their old friends again. One playtime, Sally was reading as Emma walked past.

"That's my favorite book," said Emma shyly.

"Really?" said Sally. "It's my favorite, too. I love the part when the bad dinosaur falls into the river and they fish him out in a net! That's funny!"

"I laugh at that, too," said Emma, and they chatted on until it was time for class.

After that, Sally and Emma always sat together in class, played together at playtime, and read together at reading time. And Emma did not feel so shy now that she had a special friend of her own.

THE EGG AND SPOON RACE

Walter and his friends were going in for the egg and spoon race at their school fair. They had to run along, balancing an egg on a spoon, and the first person over the finish line would win. Now, they were practicing.

Lucy held her egg straight out in front of her and ran with tiny little steps.

George carried his egg close against his chest and took great big strides.

Donna held her egg on the spoon with her thumb and raced as fast as she could.

But Walter just walked along very carefully, making sure his egg didn't fall.

"Walter's going to be last!" laughed his friends. Walter ignored them.

"On your marks, get set, go!" shouted their teacher, and the race began.

Lucy didn't look where she was going and ran around in circles.

George's egg fell off his spoon and rolled into a hole.

Donna was sent home by the teacher for cheating.

And where was Walter? Walking along very carefully—first over the finish line!

Madeleine and Isobel wanted to play in a band. They would make the instruments, learn the tunes, and put on a show. There was plenty of time—it was an hour until mealtime.

Isobel borrowed a wooden spoon, an old saucepan and two saucepan lids from her mom. Madeleine found an empty shoe box, some rubber bands, and a whistle. This was going to be easy!

A big blanket was soon spread across the grass, and the drum and cymbals placed in the middle.

Madeleine stretched the rubber bands around the shoe box, and then twanged them to test the sound.

"Just like a real guitar," she beamed. "And I'll keep the whistle in my top pocket so it's handy."

"Let's not practice," said Madeleine. "I'm sure we'll be fine." So they went to collect the audience: Isobel's mom, Auntie Millie, and baby brother Tom.

The concert was a resounding success. Tom yelled at the first song, but once they let him bang the drum, he joined in happily, and it didn't matter that he wasn't quite in time with the music. The audience said they could not wait to hear the next show—and Isobel and Madeleine couldn't wait to perform!

Peter and Leo were the best of friends. They lived close to each other, they played together, and they sometimes stayed overnight at each other's houses.

One day, though, they had a fight. It started off as a game, but Peter squeezed Leo a little too tightly and Leo butted Billy rather too hard, and before they knew it they were really hurting each other.

After that, they stopped playing together and they didn't even smile if they passed by each other. Peter felt very lonely and Leo missed Peter, too, but they didn't know how to make up.

Then one afternoon Leo was coming back from school and he saw Peter with three bigger dinosaurs. They were pulling his tail and Peter was crying.

"Leave him alone!" shouted Leo. "He's my friend."

The other dinosaurs ran off, and Peter and Leo went home together.

"I'm glad we're still friends," said Peter. "Let's not fight ever again."

Once upon a time, there was a dinosaur who set out to travel around the world in search of adventure.

So off she went, to see what there was to be seen. She climbed up great high mountains, covered in pine trees. She slithered down steep gorges and swam in icy lakes, crossed deserts, and splashed though muddy swamps.

And what amazing creatures she came across! Huge dinosaurs with legs like tree trunks that made the earth shake when they stamped along; flying dinosaurs whose scaly wings made the air rush and swirl as they soared through the sky; swimming dinosaurs who whipped the water into a froth with their enormous fins.

Then one day, she decided it was time to go home.

"Tell us what there is in the world," said the other dinosaurs when she got back. And every night they would curl up by the fire and listen to stories of amazing adventures that made their spines prickle. But they never dared go traveling themselves.

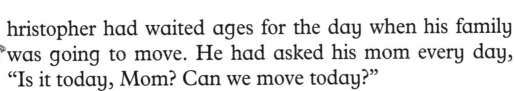

Christopher had waited ages for the day when his family was going to move. He had asked his mom every day, "Is it today, Mom? Can we move today?"

Now, at last, Christopher stood in his room, surrounded by boxes. He could hardly wait! Soon he would be in his new home.

"I'll have a last look to make sure we haven't left anything," said Mom. Christopher went with her.

"Nothing here . . . nothing there . . ." muttered his mom as she scurried from room to room.

Christopher peered into his empty room. A toy dinosaur lay abandoned on the floor. He picked it up. This was *his* room—nowhere else could be the same!

"Mom," he wailed, the tears rising, "I don't want to move!" His mom rushed to comfort him, but he spent an unhappy journey to the new house.

He picked up the smallest box and followed his parents to a large, sunny room with a big window. There was a closet in the corner which was just right for his toys, and a neat alcove for his bed.

"My bed can go here, my desk there," he grinned. "It's not the same as my old room—it's better!"

"O h, it will be splendid!" cried Esther. "Can we really look after cousin Bertie for the whole day?"

"Yes," replied Mom, "and you'll have to help us, Eric. Looking after a baby is hard work." Eric groaned.

Auntie and Uncle delivered the smiling baby. As the door closed behind them, Bertie howled.

"Come for a cuddle," suggested Esther. "Would you like a cookie? Are you thirsty?" Still Bertie yelled. Eric had had enough already. He thumped his fist on the table.

"Oh, please," he moaned. "Do we have to put up with this all day?" There was silence! Bertie looked at him then banged his little fist on the table.

"Oplzz," he mimicked, "aweggupalay!"

They played parrots and Bertie copied everything that Esther and Eric said or did. They banged saucepan lids until Mom couldn't stand it any longer. They built towers of bricks for Bertie to knock down and brought him rattles to shake. They fed the ducks at the park and swung on the swings.

By the time Bertie's parents returned, he was fed, bathed, and in his pajamas. He was fast asleep. But they had to knock loudly on the door because Mom, Esther, and Eric had all fallen asleep as well!

Arnie was a magic dinosaur. If he concentrated very hard on anything, he could change his shape and color, so that he looked like a tree, or a traffic light, or his Great Aunt Jane, who was very ugly (this was his friends favorite one). But Arnie wasn't very good at controlling his magic talent. Sometimes, when he was watching the sports on television, he would suddenly turn into a football, which always made his mom and dad drop their dinner in surprise! Other times, no matter what he did, he was just plain Arnie.

One day, on the way home from school, Arnie saw some nasty-looking men with guns and sacks stealing money from the bank. This was his big chance! He concentrated harder than ever before, and tried and tried until . . . he made himself look like Percy the Policeman! The robbers ran off frightened. Arnie got a huge reward for his magic trick, and went to a beach with all his family, where he happily concentrated on being a surfboard for two whole weeks!

85

Jane and her little brother Ricky had gone to Hayley's house. Hayley and Jane were playing, but whenever Ricky tried to join in, the girls said, "You can't play — you're too little. Go away!"

Ricky was too little to draw pictures, he was too little to go in the treehouse, and he was too little to dress up. So instead, he started to play with a ball.

He could hear Hayley's baby sister crying, but when she saw Ricky chasing the ball, she stopped.

Ricky rolled the ball across the floor and the baby rolled it back. She smiled at him.

Ricky bounced the ball and threw it up in the air with the end of his tail. The baby started to laugh.

Hayley's mother brought Ricky and the baby some juice and cookies. After that, she gave Ricky a tricycle that Hayley had grown out of. Ricky rode in circles around the baby, and she laughed and laughed.

When Jane and Hayley came in, they wanted to ride the tricycle. But Ricky said, "You're too big. Go away!"

I t was a bitterly cold winter. Maria could not remember when it had been so cold.

"Nonsense," said Grandpa. "It was colder when I was young. Once it was so cold that the lake froze, and we went skating on the ice." Maria hoped it would get that cold and she could go skating. But Grandpa always said things were better when he was young.

Each day when Grandpa returned from his walk, brushing off snow and stamping his feet, he would say, "It's not as cold as when I was a boy." For two weeks this went on, until Maria decided she would never be able to ice skate. When Grandpa came in that day, she could hardly believe what she heard.

"It's even colder than when I was a boy!"

"What was that, Grandpa?" she asked.

"You heard!" laughed Grandpa. "The ice is so thick, it is safe for the heaviest dinosaur. Let's go skating!"

What a wonderful time they had. Maria fell over many times before she got the knack, but soon they were zooming this way and that.

"That was wonderful, Grandpa," said Maria.

"It was, wasn't it?" replied Grandpa with a smile. "It was even better than when I was young!"

Kirsty and Callum had known Gemma ever since they hatched. They used to play together every week. When Gemma's family moved away, the children had been very sad. Now Gemma and her mother were coming to visit, and Kirsty and Callum were worried.

"What if we don't know what to play anymore?" asked Callum, anxiously.

"I don't think we'll like each other now that we're older," said Kirsty.

"I am sure you will get along just fine when you meet again," they were told.

Gemma bounced with excitement in the back of the car, despite her fears. Kirsty and Callum paced up and down impatiently.

"When is she coming? Is it time? Are you sure she'll like us?" they had been asking all morning.

Then—knock, knock! Here they were at last—smiling faces, hugs and kisses, cups of tea and homemade cookies. But where were the children? They had disappeared less than a minute after they had arrived.

Their moms peered around Kirsty's bedroom door. Tea things were set out on a cloth, teddy bears were arranged in neat rows around the edge, and the dinosaurs were chattering away about this and that and five dozen other things as if they had never been apart.

Rich and Andy went to the park to play soccer. It was very warm so they took off their sweaters and marked out a goal with them.

"You be goalkeeper first, Rich," said Andy.

Then he took a flying kick at the ball. BAM! It sped past Rich before he could spot it.

"Goal!" shouted Andy excitedly.

"BAM!" He soon had another goal, and another. Then Andy offered to be the goalkeeper. "Now see how many goals you can get, Rich," he said.

Rich placed the ball a short distance in front of the goal. Taking careful aim, he kicked it hard. But the ball missed the goal and landed in a trash can.

"Have another try!" said Andy.

Rich did, but the ball went wide again. However much he tried, Rich could not score a single goal.

"I'm not very good at soccer!" he sighed. Then he had an idea. Instead of kicking the ball, he swiped it with his powerful tail. The ball flew past Andy.

"Hurray! Goal! It's easier if dinosaurs play *tail*ball!" laughed Rich.

89

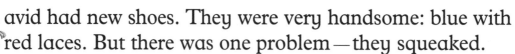

David had new shoes. They were very handsome: blue with red laces. But there was one problem—they squeaked.

As they walked to school, David tried skipping, hopping, walking slowly and quickly. Still the shoes squeaked. The mailman riding past frowned as he heard the noise and stopped to look at his bicycle.

"It's not your bike," laughed David's mom. "It's my son's shoes!" David blushed pink.

They passed a lady with a stroller. When she heard the squeak, she looked quizzically at the stroller's wheels.

"It's not your stroller," said David's mom. "It's my son's shoes!" David blushed red.

Later that morning, David was handing out the books while his teacher wrote on the blackboard.

"I hate squeaky chalk, don't you?" she said.

"It's not the chalk," muttered David. "It's my shoes." At that moment the principal walked in. Suddenly she went pale and jumped on a chair with a squeal!

"Oh no! A mouse!" she cried. David smiled his first smile of the day.

"Don't worry," he said. "It's not a mouse—it's my new shoes!"

Captain Cutlass stood on deck surrounded by his crew.

"Stick with me, men!" he cried, "We'll be the richest and the bravest pirates sailing the seas. We sail west for seven days to dig for treasure."

"We are with you, Captain!" they chorused.

But after seven storm-tossed days there was still no sign of land! The eighth day passed, and they ran out of food. The ninth day passed, and they ran out of water.

"Land ahoy!" shouted the bosun. Filled with new strength, they pulled on the oars, then leapt to shore. The Captain drew out the precious map which had never left his side. Glancing at his compass, he led them beyond the woodland, past Skull Mountain, and over the stream to the three lonely trees.

"This is where we'll find the treasure," he said.

The crew needed no second bidding. In minutes they were knee deep in a vast hole. Then their metal spades clanked against metal! They pryed the great chest from the clinging sand, their eyes gleaming. The Captain's first blow buckled the metal. With the second, the shattered padlock gave way. He lifted the creaking lid. The treasure was theirs at last!

"Well, boys," said Dad. "I'm glad you found the lunch box again. Tidy up your toys now, its time to go home. What a fun day we've had on the beach!"

Renu was a very small dinosaur who was always being bullied. She decided to invent an invisible friend who would protect her. She called him Leonard.

One day, Big Tracy invited Renu to lunch. Renu knew that Big Tracy was very greedy, and that she usually left nothing for anyone else to eat. So as soon as Renu arrived, she said, "This is my friend, Leonard. He's a cave monster. You can't see him because he is invisible, but he is VERY large and VERY fierce."

Big Tracy looked scared. "Don't worry," said Renu. "Invisible cave monsters are always good when they've had some chocolate cake."

Big Tracy quickly cut a huge slice of chocolate cake for him. Renu pretended to feed it to Leonard, but when Big Tracy wasn't looking, she gobbled it up herself.

"Leonard is growling," said Renu. "I think he's still hungry. It takes a lot to fill him up."

Big Tracy gave Leonard four more cakes, nine cookies, and six glasses of lemonade. Renu was really feeling very full!

At five o'clock Renu and Leonard politely said goodbye. "Thank you, Tracy," Renu smiled. "Leonard *is* fierce but invisible cave monsters are always good if you invite them again."

Sammy was an unhappy cat. He was always being bullied by the other dinosaurs, who liked to scare him by leaping out from behind the trees, roaring and bellowing. He became more and more timid.

One night, Sammy had the most *terrible* toothache.

"Ohhhh, ohhhh," he moaned, because his mouth ached and ached and ached.

When morning came he was very grumpy. He walked into the forest where all the dinosaurs were playing, but as soon as they saw him, they ran away.

"I wonder what they are afraid of?" thought Sammy, looking around him. Just then, he caught his reflection in the stream, and what a big surprise he got!

"So that's why the dinosaurs ran away. I've grown big, new, ferocious teeth," said Sammy. "I'll never be frightened again!"

Sammy soon managed to make new friends because no one dared bully him now that he was a ferocious saber-toothed tiger!

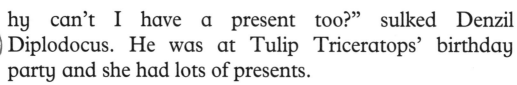

Why can't I have a present too?" sulked Denzil Diplodocus. He was at Tulip Triceratops' birthday party and she had lots of presents.

"It's not your birthday," said his dad. "When it is, you'll get lots of presents."

"Time for party games," called Tulip's mom. "All winners will get a prize!" Denzil cheered up.

They played Musical Chairs, and Darren won some candy. They played Pin the Tail on the Brontosaurus, and Katy won a raspberry lollipop. They played Pass the Package, and Josh won a toy truck.

"Not fair!" complained Denzil.

"Now let's play hunt for treasure," said Tulip, but Denzil wouldn't. He sat in a corner and sulked.

The dinosaurs hunted for the treasure all over Tulip's cave but no one could find it.

"We looked everywhere," said Tulip.

"I can see somebody's found the treasure," said Tulip's mom. "Denzil Diplodocus, come and get your prize!"

"Me?" thought Denzil, "But I haven't found the treasure." He went pink and stood up. Then he saw that he had been sitting on it all along!

Danny wanted to be a policeman. He spent all his time chasing crooks, but he had never yet caught any. One day, Danny went to visit his Uncle Dennis. After knocking loudly on the door three times, Danny wondered if his uncle was at home. He peeked through the window, and saw, to his amazement, Uncle Dennis tied up behind the sofa!

"He's been tied up by burglars!" Danny thought. "It's probably the crocodile gang from up-stream that the police have been trying to catch for ages. They're *very* fierce," he thought, excitedly.

Danny was so busy thinking about how to rescue his uncle, that he nearly leapt out of his skin when Uncle Dennis tripped over his tail. "Uncle Dennis!" he cried, "But then . . . who's tied up behind the sofa?"

"Catching crooks again, Danny?" Uncle Dennis replied. "No one's tied up behind the sofa, except a pile of my old clothes. I've been doing some cleaning up. In fact, now that you've tripped me up on my own garden path, you can help me."

"Foiled again!" groaned Danny.

Cathy had been looking forward to her birthday party for weeks. This year, a magician was going to come to the house to do all sorts of tricks and make animals out of balloons. Cathy couldn't wait! She was sitting upstairs, wearing her best dress and waiting for her friends to arrive.

Cathy crept downstairs to the kitchen, opened the door and saw all the food laid out on the table.

"No one will notice if I just eat one tiny little hot dog," thought Cathy. But before she knew it, she'd eaten hot dogs and sandwiches and potato chips and cakes, stuffing them in as fast as she could. She was just scooping a big piece of frosting off the birthday cake when she heard the doorbell ring. It was her party guests.

Cathy's friends had brought her cookies and candy, chocolate and lollipops, and her mother had cut her an extra large piece of birthday cake! Cathy really felt very sick indeed, but she had to make an effort to eat it all up. She decided that one birthday meal would be enough next year!